MOSS
GOWN

For Willy, whose mother is Candace. —W.H.H.

For Dianne Hess —D.C.

Clarion Books
a Houghton Mifflin Company imprint
215 Park Avenue South, New York, NY 10003
Text copyright © 1987 by William H. Hooks
Illustrations copyright © 1987 by Donald Carrick

For information about permission to reproduce
selections from this book, write to Permissions,
Houghton Mifflin Company, 2 Park Street, Boston, MA 02108

Printed in Japan

Library of Congress Cataloging-in Publication Data

Hooks, William H.
Moss gown.
Summary: After failing to flatter her father as
much as her two evil sisters, Candace is banished from
his plantation; and only after much time and meeting
her Prince Charming, is her father able to appreciate her
love.
[1. Fairy tales] I. Carrick, Donald, ill.
II. Title.
PZ8.H77Mo   1987   [E]   86-17199
ISBN 0-89919-460-5   PA ISBN 0-395-54793-8

DNP   10   9   8   7   6   5   4   3

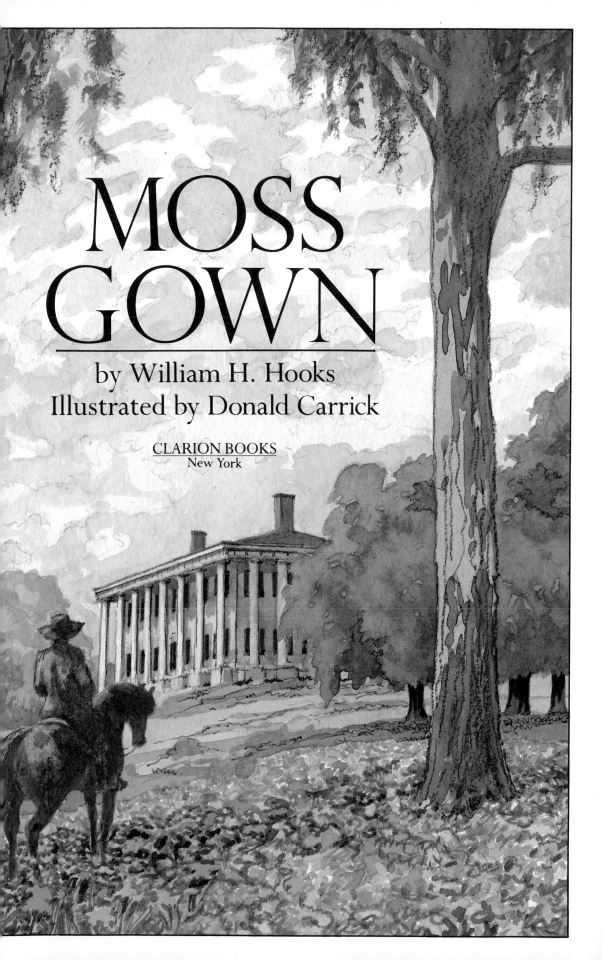

MOSS GOWN

by William H. Hooks
Illustrated by Donald Carrick

CLARION BOOKS
New York

I

Long ago in the old South there was a man
who owned a great plantation.
He lived with his three daughters
in a snow-white house,
pillared with eight marble columns
on every side.

The man grew old and sickly.
His limbs shook, and his eyesight dimmed.
He no longer delighted in riding
through his fine fields
or hunting in the mysterious swamp.
He spent his days
sitting on the wide porch
pondering what to do with his lands.

At last, one pale gray day
when a skittering wind splashed rain
against the tall columns,
the old man called to his daughters.
"Retha! Grenadine! And Candace!
Where's my little Candace?"

Retha and Grenadine, the older daughters,
peered out through the windows
and laughed at their father.
"Look at the old fool," said Retha.
"He's getting all wet," said Grenadine.

Candace, the youngest daughter,
rushed out onto the porch.
"Come inside, Father," she said.
"You're shaking in this foul wind
that blows so damp and cold."

"Summon your sisters," said the old man.
"I've a gift for each of you."

Hearing the word *gift,*
the older sisters rushed outside.
Grenadine cried, "Father, poor Father,
you're cold from the wind!"
"Shame on you, Candace!" scolded Retha.
"Letting our father get wet in the rain!"

"Please listen, my daughters,"
said the old man.
"I have pondered long
how to divide my lands.
And today the answer came."

Grenadine and Retha winked at each other
and snickered behind his back.
Candace stared lovingly
at her father.

"I have a question, my daughters:
How much do you love me?
Answer that question,
and think carefully what you say.
For I will divide my lands among you,
according to the degree of your love."

Retha and Grenadine hugged the old man,
and smothered him in fancy phrases.
"We love you," they cried,
"more than diamonds and rubies,
more than bright silver and fine gold!"

The man smiled at his older daughters.
But in his secret heart
he loved most dearly young Candace.
He waited for her words,
hoping they would be the best.

Candace knew her sisters flattered the old man
only to gain a larger gift.
She remained quiet, searching her heart
for some simple, truthful way
to say how much she loved her father.

At last she found the right words.
She took her father's hand and said,
"Father, I love you
more than meat loves salt."

"What does that mean?" said Grenadine.
"I always knew it!" shouted Retha.
"She loves our father no more than common salt."

Angry and hurt, the old man
pulled his hand away from Candace.
"Is that your answer?" he asked.

Candace struggled for words to explain.
But no words came.
The air was filled with her sisters' shrieks.
"Ungrateful!" yelled Retha.
"What a shameful thing to say to our dear father!"
cried Grenadine.

Candace held back her tears.
It broke her heart to think
that her father liked
the fancy false words of her sisters
more than the simple true words
that came from her heart.

The old man trembled
with disappointment, believing
that the daughter he had loved most
loved him as little as common salt.
He struggled to his feet
and said sternly,
"I must keep my word.
Candace will always have my love,
but all my lands
I give to Retha and Grenadine."

The sky darkened
and the wind rattled the windows.
By nightfall a hurricane
lashed the tall columns
of the great white house.

Even as the old man slept,
with troubled dreams of Candace,
Retha and Grenadine turned their sister
out into the stormy night.
"Leave this land!" they shouted.
"It belongs to us now!"

II

The cruel wind pulled at Candace
and harshly pushed her about.
But she felt strangely unafraid,
as the wind drew her closer and closer
to the murky, gray-green swamp.

A mighty blast,
howling like a hurt animal,
lifted her up and sent her flying
over the black-green cypress treetops.
She rode the wind lightly,
letting it toss her to and fro
like a floppy rag doll.

Then the wind dropped her down,
down through wet branches,
past tall rushes and tangled vines,
and set her softly
on a bed of gray Spanish moss,
deep in the heart of the swamp.

With the last of her strength,
Candace burrowed into the bed of moss
and fell into a deep sleep.
The sound of singing awakened her:

> *Gris-gris, gris-gris, grine.*
> *Who'll wear my magic gown?*
> *Gris-gris, gris-gris, grine,*
> *Who'll wear my gown so fine?*

Candace peeked through the moss,
her heart pounding with fear
at what she might see.

A slender green-eyed witch woman,
black and sleek as a velvet cat,
sat at the foot of her moss bed.
In her hand she held a gossamer gown
that glistened in the moonlight.
The black woman sang:

> *Gris-gris woman work all night,*
> *weave a gown so fine,*
> *stitch in stars and pale moonlight,*
> *Gris-gris, gris-gris, grine.*

The slender black gris-gris woman
turned her green cat's-eyes toward Candace.
"Calm your heart," she said,
"and put on this gown so fine.
It holds magic as long as
the Morning Star does shine."

Candace could only stare with wonder
at the shimmering gown.
Suddenly a cloud
passed over the moon.
A swamp bird shrieked.
Candace hid again deep in the moss bed
and lay trembling.

She heard whispered words.
"Moss Gown, if ever you need me,
say the chant, *Gris-gris, gris-gris, grine,*
and I'll be with you as sudden as
the flash of a firefly."

Then all was quiet again.
The cloud passed, and the moon shone.
Candace sat up.
The beautiful black witch woman was gone.
But the gossamer gown lay on a log,
sparkling in the moonlight.

Quickly Candace put on the gown
and started to walk.
Her feet seemed to know the way.
They were fleet and sure,
pulled by a force she could not control.
But as the Morning Star faded,
and the red sun rose,
Candace saw her beautiful gown
turn into rags and gray moss.

She reached the end of the swamp
and saw a house
as fine and grand as
the white-pillared mansion of her father.

She knocked at the door.
When the Mistress of the house
saw the girl dressed in rags and moss,
she took pity on her
and sent her to the kitchen
to help with the chores.

III

"Who are you?" asked First Cook.
Candace hesitated,
not wanting to tell them her name.
"Well!" bellowed First Cook.
"Can't you speak?"

To her surprise Candace answered,
"Moss Gown."
"A fancy name won't help you here,"
answered First Cook with a scowl.

The kitchen help gave Moss Gown
all the hardest chores.
They lent her old clothes to wear,
and she hid the drab moss dress
under her bed.

Moss Gown never smiled, or sang,
or joked with the kitchen help.
She dreamed of returning home.
How she wished she might have another chance
to tell her father how much she loved him.
She yearned to explain what she had meant when she said,
"I love you more than meat loves salt."

But as fall turned into winter,
Moss Gown gave up her dreams of returning
to a home where no one wanted her.

Then came spring, all warm and flowery.
There was great excitement in the kitchen.
"The Young Master of the house
is holding a frolic," announced First Cook.
"A three-day frolic
with picnics and balls!"

First Cook clapped her hands.
"We're *all* invited to the balls," she announced.
"Everyone?" asked Moss Gown.
"Everyone who has a ball gown,"
replied First Cook.

The first night of the frolic
all the household went to the ball.
Everyone, that is, except Moss Gown,
who had no dress to wear.

Alone in her small room,
Moss Gown tried to sleep.
But the music from the ball
teased her ears.

She thought of the wonderful balls
they had held at her father's great house.
Suddenly she remembered the witch woman's words.
She pulled the tattered gown
from under the bed,
held it in her hands and chanted,
"Gris-gris, gris-gris, grine!"

Sparkling lights like fireflies all aglow
filled the dark room.
Moss Gown blinked her eyes
and saw the gris-gris woman.
Her hand was touching the gown,
and it shimmered and glowed.

She helped Moss Gown into the dress.
"Remember, this gown holds magic
only as long as the Morning Star shines,"
said the gris-gris woman.
"Now off you go to the ball!"

Moss Gown thanked the gris-gris woman
and hurried to the ball.
When she arrived the dancers gasped,
"Who is this beautiful stranger?"
The handsome Young Master of the house
came to her with outstretched hand
and swirled her away in a dance.

"Who are you?
Where do you come from?" he asked.
Moss Gown laughed and teased,
but never told him her name
or where she came from.

When the night was danced away
and the Morning Star began to fade,
the Young Master said,
"Let me take you home
so I may learn where you live."

But Moss Gown slipped away
when the Young Master turned
to talk to the musicians.

She ran to her room
and quickly closed the door,
just as the shimmering gown
changed to moss and rags.

The next day First Cook said,
"What a sight you missed, Moss Gown.
What a beautiful lady!
And nobody knows who she is.
Pity you can't come tonight and see for yourself!"

That night, after the others left for the ball,
Moss Gown took out the poor dress.
"Gris-gris, gris-gris, grine,"
she whispered.
Before her eyes flashed the gris-gris woman,
and once more she changed the moss and rags
into a glittering gown.

Again Moss Gown ran to the ball
and danced through the night
with the Young Master.
And again, as the Morning Star
began to pale,
she slipped away.

The last night of the frolic,
Moss Gown hated to have it end.
She danced on and on
with the Young Master,
until the Morning Star faded
and the gown began turning
to rags.

In panic she cried to the Young Master,
"Look! Over there, by the window!"
When he turned away,
she fled from the ball.
The Young Master said,
"I see only the red sun
rising in the window."
But Moss Gown was gone.
"Where is my beautiful lady?" he asked.
"Did anyone see her leave?"

None of the dancers had seen Moss Gown go.
But an old woman sitting by the door said,
"No one left the ball.
No one at all!
Except a poor serving girl
dressed all in rags."

The guests drifted away.
The Young Master went off to search the countryside
for the beautiful stranger.

Many weeks passed.
At last the Young Master decided
to come home,
thinking he would never find the girl.

Through the kitchen window
Moss Gown watched the Young Master's return.
It broke her heart to see
how sad and discouraged he looked.

Moss Gown longed
to tell him who she was.
But she feared he would love
only the girl in the shimmering dress,
not poor Moss Gown
who helped in the kitchen.

Day after day the Young Master brooded.
First Cook said,
"Young Master is wasting away.
We must get him to eat something!"

Moss Gown spoke.
"Let me take supper to him tonight."
First Cook laughed and said,
"You may try,
but I doubt if you'll succeed."

At nightfall Moss Gown
hurried to her room.
She put on the ragged dress.
"Gris-gris, gris-gris, grine,"
she whispered.

Instantly the gris-gris woman was there.
"This time," she said,
"when the Morning Star fades,
do not run away."
She touched the ragged dress
and it glowed with magic light.

Moss Gown found the Young Master
still sitting on the porch.
She tapped him lightly.
"I've brought your supper," she said.
"Go away," said the Young Master
in a sad, low voice.
"Please, just take a look
at what First Cook has sent,"
pleaded Moss Gown.

The Young Master turned toward her.
"I'm dreaming," he said.
"It's you! Are you real?"
"Hush, hush," said Moss Gown.
"Eat your supper
and I'll answer your questions."

Moss Gown and the Young Master
talked on and on through the night.
Neither of them noticed
when the Morning Star paled,
and the first glimmer
of the rising sun spread over them.
The magic gown began to turn
to rags and moss.

Suddenly, Moss Gown's hand brushed against the rags.
She trembled, afraid that
the Young Master would no longer
love the girl in the tattered dress.
But she dared ask,
"How much do you love me now?"
"More than ever!"
declared the Young Master.
"Rags and tatters
could never hide your beauty!"

IV

Moss Gown and the Young Master
were married the very next week.
Friends and relatives from all over
gathered to celebrate.
At the back of the hall
two strangers appeared:
A slender black woman
with cat-green eyes,
and an old man,
feeble and almost blind.

After the wedding feast
no one could find
the woman with the cat-green eyes.
But the old man lingered,
seeming confused and lost.
The servants took him in
to warm by the kitchen fire.

The old man had been wandering for many weeks,
and he told them a tale
of two cruel daughters
who had squandered his wealth.
At last the daughters had turned him out
to sleep in the fields and beg for his food.

The next day Moss Gown saw the old man
sitting in the kitchen garden,
and she knew that he was her father.
She rushed to his side and said,
"Good Sir, do you know who I am?"

The old man squinted his eyes
and stared at her,
but he did not recognize his daughter.
"I hope you're a kind lady
who will spare an old man
a little bread and meat from your table."

Moss Gown was grieved that
her father did not recognize her.
"You are welcome in my house,
good Sir," she replied.
She hurried to the kitchen.
"First Cook," she called,
"make a special dinner tonight,
and leave the salt out of everything."

First Cook was puzzled,
but she prepared the meal.

Moss Gown had her father
seated next to her
at the long dinner table.
When he tasted the food,
he frowned and pushed his plate away.
Moss Gown handed him a saltcellar.
"Here," she said softly.
And then she added,
"I love you
more than meat loves salt."

The old man looked up,
his eyes seemed to clear for a moment,
and he recognized his daughter.
"My long-lost Candace!" he cried,
reaching for her hand.
"How I misjudged you!
How I have missed you!"

"Those are the words I have so longed to hear,"
said Candace. And she hugged her father.

The Young Master invited the old man
to stay with them as long as he liked.
There was rejoicing and dancing
in the great house that night.

"Candace is a pretty name,"
said the Young Master to his bride
as they danced.
"But Moss Gown will always be
my name for you."
Then he whispered in Candace's ear,
"I love you, Moss Gown,
more than meat loves salt."

Author's Note

Moss Gown is based on stories I heard as a child growing up in the tidewater section of eastern North Carolina. This area has preserved through its lively tradition of storytelling many elements of Elizabethan culture. It was here that the first English colony in America was established in the sixteenth century; and it was the birthplace of Virginia Dare, the first English child born on American soil. So it is not surprising that elements of the King Lear story and *Cinderella* should have been preserved in the oral tradition. What is remarkable about *Moss Gown* is how these elements over the years became blended into a single story.

Another version of the *Moss Gown* tale thrives with the storytellers of Appalachia in western North Carolina, who are descended from the same English stock as the coastal settlers of the tidewater region. Their version of the story is called *Rush Cape.* Since Spanish moss did not grow in the mountains of Appalachia, the heroine of the story is given a cape of rushes as a magical dress, rather than the enchanted gown of moss.

The term *gris-gris* (pronounced "gree-gree") is French and was used in the Carolinas to identify a kind of spell-casting—often dire and evil in its intent. Sometimes the spell could be positive and good, as in the case of *Moss Gown;* but it was always a powerful, magical force.